A Note from Michelle about
MY LIFE IS A THREE-RING CIRCUS

Hi! I'm Michelle Tanner. I'm nine years old. You'll never guess what I'm doing this summer. I'm going to circus camp!

And at the end of camp, I'm going to be in a big circus show with all the other kids. I can already see myself swinging on the trapeze in a sparkling pink costume. My whole family will be cheering for me—and that's a lot of people!

There's my dad and my two older sisters, D.J. and Stephanie. But that's not all.

My mom died when I was little. So my uncle Jesse moved in to help Dad take care of us. So did Joey Gladstone. He's my dad's friend from college. It's almost like having three dads. But that's still not all!

First Uncle Jesse got married to Becky Donaldson. Then they had twin boys, Nicky and Alex. The twins are four years old now. And they're so cute.

That's nine people. And our dog, Comet, makes ten. Sure, it gets kind of crazy sometimes. But I wouldn't change it for anything. It's so much fun living in a full house!

FULL HOUSE™ MICHELLE novels

Available from MINSTREL Books

FULL HOUSE™
Michelle

My Life Is a Three-Ring Circus

Cathy East Dubowski

A Parachute Book

Published by POCKET BOOKS
New York   London   Toronto   Sydney   Tokyo   Singapore

A MINSTREL PAPERBACK *Original*

A Minstrel Book published by
POCKET BOOKS, a division of Simon & Schuster Inc.
1230 Avenue of the Americas, New York, NY 10020

A PARACHUTE BOOK

Copyright © and ™ 1998 by Warner Bros.

FULL HOUSE, characters, names and all related indicia are trademarks of Warner Bros. © 1998.

ISBN: 0-671-01730-6

First Minstrel Books printing June 1998

10 9 8 7 6 5 4 3 2 1

A MINSTREL BOOK and colophon are registered trademarks of Simon & Schuster Inc.

Cover photo by Schultz Photography

Printed in the U.S.A.

My Life Is a Three-Ring Circus

Chapter
1

♥ "I won! I won!" Nine-year-old Michelle Tanner ran in the front door of her house, waving a ripped-open envelope.

No one answered. No one came running to hear her big news.

Even her dog Comet didn't budge. He just opened an eye and thumped his tail once.

Michelle frowned. She lived in an old Victorian house with eight other people. There were her father, Danny, and her two sisters—eighteen-year-old D.J. and thirteen-year-old Stephanie.

Her uncle Jesse and aunt Becky and their

four-year-old twin boys, Nicky and Alex, lived on the third floor. And Joey Gladstone, her dad's best friend, had an apartment in the basement.

Joey and Jesse moved in after Michelle's mother died. They wanted to help out. Michelle was just a baby back then. She couldn't remember a time when Joey and Jesse hadn't been around.

It was definitely a full house! So where was everybody?

Michelle smiled. *I* know how to get their attention! she thought. She ran to the front door and opened it. She rang the bell.

Ding-dong!

"Pizza's here!" she shouted at the top of her lungs.

A split second later Stephanie and D.J. pounded down the stairs, followed by Uncle Jesse. He was followed by the twins, who were chased by Aunt Becky.

Joey bolted up the stairs from his basement apartment.

Michelle's dad hurried in from the kitchen, wiping his hands on a dish towel. "Pizza!" he exclaimed. "Who ordered pizza? I've got a casserole in the oven."

Michelle grinned as the whole gang stared at her. "Don't worry, Dad. There's no pizza. I was just trying to get everybody's attention."

"No pizza?" D.J. complained.

"We want pizza! We want pizza!" Nicky and Alex chanted.

Joey turned around and headed for the kitchen.

"Hey! Where are you going?" Michelle cried. "Don't you want to hear my news?"

"I'm going to order the pizza you promised my stomach," Joey explained.

"But what about my casserole?" Danny demanded.

Uncle Jesse put an arm around his shoulders. "Just pop it in the fridge for tomorrow night."

"But you never eat leftovers," Aunt Becky reminded him.

They were doing it again! Michelle thought. Ignoring her! She climbed up on the coffee table.

"Okay, okay," Joey said, holding up his hands. "Let's take a vote. Everybody who wants pizza say—"

"What about my news?" Michelle hollered. Everybody stopped talking.

"Don't stand on the coffee table, sweetheart," Danny said, lifting her down. "Now, what is your news?"

Michelle smiled and held up her letter. She cleared her throat. "I won! I won!" she repeated. "I'm going to circus camp!"

"Circus camp?" Danny asked. "What's that?"

"Remember, Dad?" Michelle said. "I filled out an entry form when we went to the circus last winter."

Michelle loved the circus. Especially the trapeze artists. They were so beautiful, and so brave. They flew through the air like birds from a fairy tale!

"Now I remember," Danny said. He took the letter and quickly read it. "It looks like she's really won," he told the family.

"Oh, Michelle, that's wonderful!" Aunt Becky said.

Stephanie read the letter over her father's shoulder. "I'm so jealous. You're going to learn how to be a real circus performer. And you get to be in a big show at the end of camp."

Michelle closed her eyes. She could see it now. . . .

A huge crowd filled the circus tent. Michelle stepped into the spotlight wearing a sparkling pink costume. She waved to her fans and started to climb the tall ladder leading up to the trapeze.

Finally she reached the small platform high above the net. She took the trapeze bar in both hands and swung out over the net. The crowd ooohed and aaahed.

Michelle somersaulted into the air. She was flying!

The crowd gasped. Then everyone broke into cheers as Michelle caught the bar swinging toward her from the other side of the circus ring.

"Michelle! Michelle!"

The audience loved her. They were calling her name!

"Michelle!"

Fingers snapped inches from her nose.

"Huh?" Michelle mumbled.

"Earth to Michelle," Stephanie said with a giggle. "I said—when do you go?"

"Camp starts the first week after school gets out. And it lasts two whole weeks," Michelle told them. She shot her father a worried look. "I can go—can't I? It's really close to home."

Danny smiled. "It sounds like an educational experience to me," he said.

Michelle sighed in relief. When Dad said

"educational," she knew her chances were good.

"I'll have to talk to the people running the camp," Danny said. "I want to make sure that it's safe. If everything checks out, then, yes, you may go."

"Yippee!" Michelle squealed. She twirled around the living room. "Just wait till I tell everybody at school."

"And there's a big show at the end of camp. You're all invited to come see me on the trapeze!" Michelle exclaimed.

Half the kids on the playground were gathered around Michelle. They all wanted to hear about circus camp.

"It sounds awesome. Michelle Tanner—circus star," Cassie Wilkins cried.

"I'm going to be in the front row for your show," Mandy Metz promised.

Cassie and Mandy were Michelle's two best friends. It would be weird spending two weeks at circus camp without them.

On the other hand, it would be great doing her trapeze act for them when the campers put on their own circus show.

"You're going for only two weeks," her friend Lee Wagner said. "How are you going to learn to be a trapeze artist that fast?"

Michelle folded her arms. "Natural talent!"

Mandy and Cassie giggled. But Lee shook his head. "I know you're good in sports. But I don't think *anyone* could learn to be a trapeze artist in two weeks," Lee said. "I bet you fifty bucks you won't get off the ground."

Michelle's eyes popped open. "You've got fifty dollars?"

"Well, not that I can spend," Lee admitted. "My dad made me put it in my college fund."

"I *know* I'm going to be on the trapeze," Michelle said. "So let's bet something else."

"Like what?" Lee asked.

"Like anything," Michelle said. "You pick—because you're going to lose."

"I know," Lee said. "The pool will be open when you get home from camp, right?"

"Sure," Michelle said. "It will be open all summer."

"Here's my bet, then," Lee said. "The loser has to spend one whole day at the pool—"

"What's so horrible about that?" Cassie asked.

"You didn't let me finish," Lee said. "The loser has to spend one whole day at the pool—wearing pajamas and carrying a teddy bear!"

Chapter

2

♥ "I've been waiting to start circus camp forever," Michelle told her dad.

Danny laughed. "I know it feels that way. But it's only been a month since you won the contest."

He pulled the car up to a chain-link fence. The fence went around a building that looked like a big storage warehouse.

Michelle frowned. "Are you sure this is the right place?" she asked. "It doesn't look like a circus to me."

A security guard hurried up to the front gate. He had a round red nose, bright blue hair, and the biggest shoes Michelle had ever seen. His name tag said HI, MY NAME IS CHUCKLES!

The security guard was a clown!

Michelle giggled. *"Now* it looks like a circus," she said.

Chuckles pulled a few feet of chain from his pocket. Then a few more feet. Then a few *more* feet. At the end of the long, long chain was a key. He turned it in the lock and pushed open the gate.

"Howdy, folks!" Chuckles called.

"Howdy yourself, Chuckles," Danny answered. "This is my daughter, Michelle Tanner. She's one of your campers."

Chuckles studied his jumbo-sized clipboard. "Oh, you're our lucky contest winner. Congratulations!"

"Thanks." Michelle grinned at him.

"The dormitories are around back. You're in number three," Chuckles said. "Just follow the red arrows."

Danny drove through the big gates.

11

Chuckles waved. He squeezed his red nose, and it honked like a car horn.

Michelle stared at the huge main building as they drove past. It's tall enough for the trapeze, she thought. Maybe that's where I'll be rehearsing for the big show.

"There's number three," Danny announced. He parked in front of a long metal trailer.

"Cool!" Michelle exclaimed. She thought she would be staying in a wooden cabin— like the ones at the camp she went to last summer. She loved the shiny silver trailer.

"Take a picture of me, Dad!" she exclaimed. She posed in front of the trailer.

Danny snapped her photo, then they headed inside. A dark-haired girl around D.J.'s age hurried up to them. "I bet you're Michelle Tanner," she said.

"How did you know?" Michelle asked.

"Because all the other girls have checked in," she answered. "I'm Janine, your counselor."

Janine led Michelle over to a bed covered with a bright orange bedspread. "You're right here, next to Naomi," she said.

Naomi smiled from her spot on the next bed. She had short, curly brown hair. She was wearing a long pink T-shirt over light blue leggings.

"We're almost twins," Michelle said. She had on a long light blue T-shirt over pink leggings. Pink and blue were her very favorite colors.

"While you talk to your twin, I'll go get your stuff," her dad told Michelle.

Michelle and Naomi giggled.

"I can't wait for our classes to start, can you?" Naomi asked. "I've been dreaming about this for a long time."

"Me, too," Michelle said. "I told my friends at school about it. And I invited them all to our big show."

"I invited *everyone* from school. Even kids I don't know." Naomi laughed.

The trailer door swung open, and Michelle's dad shoved his way inside. He dropped one big suitcase and one little suitcase on the floor by Michelle's bed.

"I'll leave you two to settle in together," Danny told Michelle. He gave her a kiss. "See you in two weeks."

Michelle felt a tiny bit sad. Two weeks was a very long time to spend away from her family.

"Call us whenever you feel like it," her dad said. That made Michelle feel a lot better.

"Bye, Dad," she said. "Next time you see me I'll be up on the trapeze!"

Her dad glanced at Janine. "You use nets, don't you?" he asked.

"Nets *and* safety harnesses," Janine promised him.

"Okay," he said. "Have fun, pumpkin," he told Michelle. Then he hurried out the door.

Michelle unzipped her suitcase and started unpacking.

I'm really here, she thought. She felt a shiver of excitement run through her. Her circus dream was about to come true!

Michelle ate her last bite of hamburger and grinned at Naomi.

It was so cool eating dinner in the big circus cafeteria. All the circus performers ate with the kids. The performers would be teaching the classes, too.

Janine told Michelle and Naomi that twice a year all the circus people took a break from performing and taught classes at circus camp.

"Greetings, campers," a tall, slim man called from the front of the cafeteria. He had a very loud, very deep voice. "Welcome to the Golden State Circus Camp—the greatest circus camp on earth!"

"I think he's the ringmaster for the circus," Naomi whispered.

Michelle giggled. "I could tell."

"We hope you're all as excited to be here

as we are to have you here," he said. Michelle clapped and cheered along with the other campers.

"During your first week, you will take classes in each of the different circus arts," the ringmaster said. "You'll get a taste of what it's like to be animal trainers, clowns, and trapeze artists, just to name a few."

Yes! Michelle thought. She couldn't wait.

"At the end of the week, all your teachers will get together and decide what each of you will do in our big show. Then you'll spend the next week rehearsing," the ringmaster explained.

"Does anyone have any questions?" he asked.

Michelle raised her hand. "What if you already know what you want to do?" she asked. "Can you just go to one class?"

"Good question," the man answered. "Every camper will take all the classes. A real circus artist must be able to do many things. Especially in a smaller circus. Sometimes one performer has to substitute for another."

He smiled at the group. "Trying different things also helps you find the thing that you do best. It's just like at school. You study math and English and science and art— many subjects, not just one."

Michelle nodded. It made sense. Also, it might be fun to learn some other circus stuff—as long as she got to be on the trapeze for the show.

Chapter 3

❤ On their way back to the dorms, Michelle and Naomi passed the big building that looked like a warehouse.

Naomi grabbed Michelle's arm. "There's a whole circus tent *inside* the building!" she exclaimed.

Michelle and Naomi hurried over to the huge open doorway and peered in.

"Wow!" Michelle gasped as she stepped inside. It looked just like the circus she had gone to with her dad.

There were rows and rows of bleachers and three big rings, where the circus performers did their acts. Michelle remembered trying to watch all three rings at once. The acts were so exciting, she didn't want to miss a second of any of them.

Naomi grabbed Michelle's arm. "Look!" she whispered. She pointed to a spot high above the three rings.

A blond girl about Michelle's age was practicing on the trapeze. A blond boy who looked a couple of years older was rehearsing with her.

Michelle couldn't stop staring at the girl. She flew through the air like a bird. It looked so easy. Michelle itched to get up there and try it herself.

"That's what I want to do," Michelle whispered.

"That's Katrina and Alexi Novak," Naomi whispered back. "Their whole family does a trapeze act for the circus. My mother read about them. They say Katrina and Alexi started flying almost before they started walking!"

"Wow!" Michelle said again. She couldn't wait to get on the trapeze. After watching Katrina and Alexi, she knew she would have to work really hard. She couldn't wait to start, though. She had to be great for the big show!

Michelle sat on the bleachers inside the big circus tent. Her first class was about to begin.

There were about the same number of kids in her circus class as in her regular fourth-grade class. I bet we'll have a lot of great acts for our show, she thought.

A young man with dark brown hair hurried up to them. "I'm Charley," he said. "Today I'm going to teach you the most exciting circus act."

Michelle crossed her fingers. That could be the trapeze, she thought.

"Juggling!" Charley announced.

Michelle let out a little sigh, and Charley winked at her.

"Some of you might not think juggling is that exciting," he said. "But it is when you juggle these."

Charley pulled three sharp axes out of the bag at his feet. He threw them into the air and began to juggle them. The shiny blades glistened as they whirled through the air.

"Cool!" Naomi whispered from her seat next to Michelle.

Charley returned the axes to the ground. "Since it's your first day, we'll start slowly." He passed out three soft bean-bag balls to everyone in the class.

"This should be easy," Michelle said. She jumped up and tossed the balls into the air. *Thump, thump, thump.* They all landed at her feet.

Michelle heard more thumps as balls fell to the floor all around her.

"No, no, no," Charley said with a laugh. "Trying to juggle three balls from the beginning is the wrong way to start," he said.

"That's why so many people give up. It's best to start with one ball."

"One ball?" Michelle said. "How do you juggle one ball?"

"Watch me," Charley said. He stood in a relaxed pose with his elbows pressed against his sides and his hands held up in front of him.

He tossed one ball up in the air. It made a perfect half circle as it traveled from his right hand to his left.

"Focus on tossing the ball—not catching it," Charley said. "Each time, think up, up, up. Good throws make catching easy. Also, don't catch the ball with your fingers. Catch it in the palm of your hand."

Michelle tried to stand exactly the way Charley had. She moved her feet farther apart and pressed her elbows against her sides.

Then she tossed the ball up into the air. Up, up, up, she thought.

Thud! It fell to the ground before it got halfway to her other hand.

I need to throw it a little harder, she thought. Michelle hurled the ball into the air.

"Ow!" Naomi exclaimed.

The ball had bounced off Naomi's head and dropped to the floor.

"Oops. Sorry," Michelle said.

She picked up her ball and tried one more time. *Thud!* Then again. *Thud!*

"If you're ready, try two balls," Charlie said. "Toss the first ball. Wait until it begins its arc down, then toss the second ball."

Michelle tossed one ball, then the other. *Thunk!* The balls smacked into each other in the air, then thumped to the ground. *Thud! Thud!*

"I wish my dog Comet were here," Michelle said.

"Your dog?" Naomi asked. "How come?"

"So he could fetch some of the balls I keep dropping," Michelle answered.

"Don't worry, Michelle," Naomi said. "We'll figure it out."

Michelle shrugged. "It's okay if I'm not a good juggler," she said. "You don't have to juggle on the trapeze."

Naomi looked worried. "But what if you don't get chosen for the trapeze?"

Oh, no! Michelle hadn't thought of that. She had to get chosen for the trapeze. *She just had to!* It was the only thing she wanted to do. Nothing else even came close.

Chapter 4

♥ "I am Madame Florence," an older lady told them. She had a ring on every finger and three necklaces around her neck. "Today I'm going to teach you the most thrilling circus act."

The trapeze, Michelle thought. She wanted her chance to prove to everyone that she should be on the trapeze for the big show.

It was a little hard to picture Madame Florence flying through the air, though. All her jewelry would weigh her down!

"The trained dog act," Madame Florence continued. "Meet Girard and Fifi."

Two white poodles ran up to Madame Florence and sat in front of her. Fifi was dressed like an Indian princess with a tiny feathered headdress, and Gerard was dressed like a lumberjack.

"Aren't they cute?" Michelle whispered to Naomi.

Naomi smiled and nodded.

Madame Florence led the class over to a poodle-size obstacle course in one of the circus tent's three rings. "I need a volunteer to work with Fifi and Gerard," she said.

Lots of kids raised their hands. Michelle raised her hand, too. She loved playing with Comet. Working with the poodles would be fun.

Madame Florence picked a tall boy with straight black hair. "Introduce yourself to Fifi and Gerard."

"I'm Chris," he told the dogs.

"The first thing you need to do is give Fifi and Gerard the command to start," Madame

Florence told Chris. "All you have to do is say *'allez.'* That means 'go' in French."

"Al-ay," Michelle muttered to herself. She wanted to be ready when it was her turn.

"Then, when Fifi and Gerard run over the little wooden bridge, you hold up that hoop for them to jump through," Madame Florence continued. She showed Chris the hoop.

"And when the poodles reach the end of the course, you wave the checkered flag." Madame Florence pointed to the flag lying on the floor.

"Start when you're ready," she said.

Michelle watched carefully as Chris took the poodles through the obstacle course.

After Chris, Madame Florence picked a girl named Teena. Teena seemed a little shy. Her voice was very, very soft. Fifi and Gerard didn't even hear her the first time she said *allez!*

When it was Michelle's turn, she knelt down next to Gerard and Fifi and gave them

27

each a pat on the head. Their hair felt soft and springy under her fingers.

Then she stood up. She waited until both poodles were looking at her. *"Allez!"* she cried in a loud voice.

Gerard and Fifi took off through the obstacle course. They wove around little plastic barrels. They scrambled over miniature fallen logs. Then they dashed over the miniature bridge. Their toenails made a clicking sound as they ran.

When they reached the other side, Michelle held up the big wooden hoop. Gerard and Fifi leaped through the hoop without pausing for a moment.

Michelle ran to the end of the course and picked up the checkered flag. She held the flag high over her head—and swished it down as soon as the poodles passed her.

Then she decided to add a touch of her own. She spun around in a circle. "Come on, get the flag!" she called.

Fifi and Gerard chased after the flag, leaping and barking. Everyone in the class applauded.

Madame Florence hurried up to Michelle. "The dogs can sense that you understand them and that you are their friend. They will do things for you."

Madame Florence picked up Fifi and Gerard and cuddled them in her arms. "Ah, you like Michelle, no?" Madame Florence asked the poodles.

Michelle grinned.

"Would you like to perform with her in the big show?" Madame Florence asked the dogs.

Uh-oh! Michelle thought. She liked Fifi and Gerard a lot, it was fun to work with them. She couldn't do a dog act in the big show, though. She just couldn't.

She had to fly on the trapeze! She'd been dreaming about it ever since she won the contest.

Besides, she'd lose her big bet with Lee if she wasn't a trapeze artist in the show. And all her friends in school and her family were coming to see her—*on the trapeze!*

What am I going to do? Michelle thought. I already proved to Madame Florence that I'm good at working with Fifi and Gerard.

Madame Florence handed Fifi to Michelle. One of the feathers on Fifi's Indian headdress tickled Michelle's nose.

That was it!

Michelle turned away from Madame Florence. Then she leaned down and brushed her nose back and forth across the feather headdress.

"Ah-choo!" she sneezed.

No one seemed to notice.

Michelle rubbed her nose across the feathers again.

"Ah-choo! Ah-choo! Ah-choo!"

"Are you all right?" Madame Florence asked.

"I don't know," Michelle fibbed. "I think I'm allergic to your dogs." Michelle gently returned Fifi to the floor.

"But, Michelle," Naomi called, "I thought you said you have a dog at home."

"Well, uh—maybe I'm just allergic to poodles," Michelle said quickly.

Madame Florence just laughed. "I do not think that is possible," she said. "Perhaps it is just dust."

Then Madame Florence gave a tiny frown. "I hope you are not coming down with something. It would be a shame if you had to miss the big show."

Chapter

5

♥ Michelle and Naomi hurried to the circus tent the next morning.

Madame Florence gave them a big smile on her way out. "Michelle, how are you feeling?"

"Great!" Michelle exclaimed. "Totally wonderful!"

Michelle almost blew it with all her sneezing the day before. She didn't want Madame Florence to think she was getting sick.

"I will tell Gerard and Fifi you said hello," Madame Florence told her. She waved good-bye.

Michelle and Naomi joined the rest of their class. A muscular man strode over to them. His red hair shone under the lights.

"I'm Daniel," he announced. "Today I'm going to teach you the most spectacular circus act."

Is it finally time for the trapeze? Michelle wondered.

"Bareback riding!" Daniel continued.

"Oh, I love horses!" Naomi squealed.

"Me, too," Michelle answered.

"Who wants to go first?" Daniel asked.

Naomi's hand shot up.

"Okay, come and meet Spotty," Daniel said. A teenage girl led a horse to the front of the center ring. It was white with black spots that reminded Michelle of spattered paint.

Spotty was the biggest horse Michelle had ever seen. She gave a hard gulp.

Michelle watched as Daniel hooked a safety belt around Naomi's waist and helped her up on Spotty.

"Today you're all going to get a chance to try standing up on Spotty's back while he walks around the ring," Daniel told them. "Just think of Spotty as a big surfboard."

Whoa, Michelle thought. That sounds a little scary.

She held her breath as Daniel began to lead Spotty around the ring. On her second trip around, Naomi pushed herself to her knees. Then, carefully, slowly, she stood up.

"Yay! Naomi!" Michelle called out.

Michelle watched her friend balance with her arms out to the sides. It did sort of look like surfing! Michelle and the other kids clapped and clapped.

Naomi began to wobble. Michelle gasped as Naomi started to fall off the horse.

Daniel's assistants were quick. They pulled on the safety lines attached to Naomi's harness. Instead of falling, Naomi swung in the air above the ground.

Daniel's assistants lowered her to her feet

and then Daniel unhooked her. "Wonderful!" Daniel exclaimed. "You're a natural."

Naomi ran back to Michelle. "Oh, Michelle, that was so cool!"

"You were awesome," Michelle said.

Daniel picked another girl to try bareback riding.

"Her ponytail is almost as long as Spotty's," Naomi joked.

"Maybe I should try to grow my hair longer," Michelle said. "Her hair looks really pretty."

Michelle noticed that it took the girl a little longer than it had taken Naomi to work her way onto her feet.

"It looked a lot easier when you were up there," Michelle told her.

"I've been taking gymnastics since I was five, which helped," Naomi said. "Spotty's back was sort of like the balance beam—but wider."

"Why don't you go next," Daniel called

to Michelle after he helped the girl with the ponytail out of her safety gear.

Michelle ran into the ring. She didn't feel as nervous after watching Naomi. Riding standing up looked kind of like fun.

I just have to remember not to do *too* well, Michelle thought. I don't want the teachers picking me as the bareback rider for the show.

Daniel hooked the safety belt around Michelle's waist. He helped Michelle onto Spotty's back. Whoa! Spotty seemed even bigger up close! She grabbed on tight to his mane.

Daniel's eyebrows shot up. "Have you ever been on a horse?" he whispered.

"Yes," Michelle said. "But they weren't this big. Also, they had saddles."

"Don't worry. We'll take it very slowly." Then he started Spotty around the ring. "Just get used to the horse's rhythm. Remember, the horse is your friend."

Michelle nodded and forced herself to let

go of Spotty's mane. She hoped she wouldn't fall off!

"When you're ready, try to get up on your knees," Daniel said.

Michelle took a deep breath. She leaned forward, close to Spotty's neck. She tried to bring one leg up under her.

Daniel grabbed her ankle and helped her move her leg into position. She managed to slide her other leg under her without help.

"Stay like that for a moment and try to find your balance," Daniel coached. "Then, when you're ready, try standing up."

Spotty's gentle rocking motion made balancing on her knees easier than Michelle expected.

Slowly, slowly, Michelle rose into a crouch. Then she froze.

She couldn't stand up—and she couldn't sit back down. Her knees started to tremble.

"Whoaaa!" Michelle tumbled off the side of the horse!

Daniel's assistants pulled on the safety lines and Michelle swung into the air.

Her stomach churned as she watched the ground twirl beneath her. Spotty kicked sawdust into her eyes and nose as he trotted away.

Daniel helped her get to her feet and unhooked her. Michelle's heart wouldn't stop pounding, and she knew her face was bright red.

"Good try!" Daniel said. "Want to go again?"

Michelle gulped some air. "Uh, I think I'll let somebody else have a turn."

I guess I don't have to worry about being picked as the show's bareback rider, Michelle thought. Trapeze—here I come!

Chapter 6

♥ Yes! The moment Michelle saw her teachers she knew this was the big day. The day she would get her chance on the trapeze.

The blond girl and boy Michelle had seen rehearsing on the trapeze her first day were now standing in front of the class. A blond man and woman stood beside them.

"I am Mr. Novak," the man said. "And this is Mrs. Novak, Katrina, and Alexi. Together we are the Amazing Novak Family. Today we are going to teach you the most dazzling circus act."

"The trapeze!" Michelle blurted out.

"That's right!" Mr. Novak exclaimed.

Michelle was ready. She could already see herself—the star of the show—dressed in a sparkling pink costume, flying above the crowd. . . .

Mr. Novak began a little talk about the history of trapeze artists. Michelle tried to pay attention, but it was hard. She had already waited so long.

Then Mrs. Novak gave the class a safety lesson. And Katrina and Alexi demonstrated how to fall into the net safely.

Michelle was a lot more interested in flying than falling. But she listened carefully, anyway.

"Who wants to go first?" Mr. Novak called out. Katrina and Mrs. Novak and Alexi started up the ladder to the platform above the net.

Michelle jumped to her feet and raised her hand. "Me! Please! Please!"

Mr. Novak smiled. "An eager student, I

see. Well, come on. You will be the first little birdie to leave the nest."

The class laughed.

Michelle hurried to the bottom of the ladder. She gazed up into the ropes and wires crisscrossing the ceiling. Katrina, Alexi, and Mrs. Novak stood on the platform above.

Even though Mr. Novak explained that they had lowered the platform for the beginners' class, it seemed high to Michelle.

Mr. Novak hooked a safety belt to her waist. Safety lines were hooked to each side of the belt. Assistants held the end of each rope.

"Now you're ready," Mr. Novak said.

Michelle put one foot on the bottom rung of the ladder. She took a deep breath, but suddenly she found that she couldn't move.

"Up you go now," Mr. Novak said cheerfully. "I'm right behind you. Katrina and Mrs. Novak will help you at the top." Michelle started up the ladder.

With each step, she felt a little more nervous.

"That's it," Mr. Novak said. "Just one step at a time. And don't look down."

Michelle looked down.

WHOOOAAA! She was already way higher than the tree house in her backyard!

She shook her head and gazed up at the platform. You'll get used to it, she told herself. Just get to the top, and you'll be fine.

She climbed another step. Then another and another and another. I'm doing it, she thought.

At last she reached the tiny platform. Katrina and Mrs. Novak grabbed her hands and helped her on.

"I'll watch you fly from the ground, little birdie," Mr. Novak said. He started back down the ladder.

The platform was barely large enough to hold Michelle, Mrs. Novak, Katrina, and Alexi. I'd better not sneeze today, Michelle thought. I might fall off.

Alexi grabbed the bar and swung himself over to the opposite platform. He waved to Michelle, and she waved back.

Then she looked down again. The safety net was there to catch her if anything went wrong. But it looked as if it were a million miles away!

Michelle squeezed her eyes shut. She knew everyone was staring at her.

Then she felt a gentle hand on her arm. When she opened her eyes, she saw Katrina smiling at her. "Don't worry," she whispered. "You don't have to do anything scary. This is just beginner stuff."

That made Michelle feel a little better. "Like juggling with just one ball, right?" Michelle said.

Then she remembered how all the bean-bag balls had hit the ground.

"Now, today we will just 'meet' the trapeze," Mrs. Novak said. "No tricks. Easy."

Michelle tried to smile. Katrina and her

family were so nice. None of this felt the way she thought it would, though.

Alexi sent the trapeze bar flying toward them. Mrs. Novak caught it. She held it in front of Michelle. "Here you go. Hold on to the bar with both hands with an overhand grasp." She placed her hands on the bar to show Michelle what she meant.

"When you are ready, you'll just go for a little ride. Katrina and I will swing you out over the net. And we'll catch you when you swing back to the platform."

"All you have to do is hang on," Katrina said. "We'll do the rest."

She dusted Michelle's hands with a white powder. "This is chalk. It helps keep your hands from slipping."

Michelle gulped. "Slipping?"

Mrs. Novak laughed. "Even we experienced trapeze artists get sweaty hands. Don't worry, honey. You'll be fine."

Michelle nodded and took the trapeze in her hands. It was about as big around as a broom handle and three feet wide. A wire attached to each end led up toward the top of the tent.

It looks like a swing in a giant bird cage, she thought and gave a nervous giggle.

Michelle felt a hand on her back and panicked. "Don't push!" she squeaked.

"Don't worry," Mrs. Novak said. "We are here to make it easy for you. You fly when you are ready."

Fly. Michelle wished she had wings right now. Then it would be easy to fly across to the other side.

She felt as heavy as a ton of bricks.

She licked her lips. "Okay, I'm almost ready."

"Just pretend it's a swing at the playground," Alexi hollered from the opposite platform.

Michelle took another deep breath. She was excited—and scared at the same time. Everyone's waiting, she told herself. Everyone's watching. Don't be a baby. You have to go. Now!

She adjusted her grip on the bar. She took another deep breath. "Okay, I'm ready," she said. She could hear her voice shaking.

"All right," Katrina said. "One . . . two—"

"Stop!" Michelle cried.

She glanced down—and felt as if she were going to throw up.

She dropped the bar and buried herself in Mrs. Novak's arms. "I can't do it! I can't!"

Chapter
7

♥ "So you got scared. It's no big deal," Naomi told Michelle.

They sat in the bleachers the next day, waiting for their teacher to arrive.

"Everyone at least *tried*," Michelle answered. "I'd been waiting for my chance on the trapeze ever since I found out I was coming here. Then I blew it!"

"Mr. Novak said you shouldn't be upset," Naomi reminded her. "He said some people are just scared of heights. Acrophobia— that's what he called it."

"Maybe I can get a job sweeping up after

the elephants," Michelle muttered. "That would keep me close to the ground."

"Hey, here comes our teacher," Naomi said. "I wonder what we'll be learning today."

Michelle sighed. What did it matter? The only thing she really wanted to be was a trapeze artist. That she messed up.

She gave a little groan. What would all her friends and family think?

"I am Mr. Hackman," the teacher announced. "But you can call me *on the phone.*" The pink flower on the brim of his hat drooped—then popped back up.

Naomi snorted.

Michelle gave a tiny smile. I'll have to remember that joke for Joey, she thought. Maybe he can use it in his stand-up comedy act.

"Today I'm going to teach you the most wonderful circus act," Mr. Hackman said. "Clowning!"

He stared at the class and shook his head.

The flower on his hat drooped again. "This group is much too sad looking. We need more laughter!"

Mr. Hackman opened up a big black trunk that stood near a tall mirror. Michelle could see that the trunk was filled with clothing.

Next he put a cardboard box on the table, along with a creased and dented black top hat turned upside down. "I'd like each of you to come up with a costume. Use anything you like from the trunk."

Mr. Hackman reached into the cardboard box and pulled out what looked like a small red rubber ball. "Then take a nose and put it on." He stuck the nose on a boy in the front of the group.

"Next pull out one slip of paper from the hat. The paper will have the title of a skit. Your job is to use the skit idea to make us laugh," Mr. Hackman continued.

"Most circus clowns don't talk when they perform," he added. "But for our first lesson, go ahead and talk if it helps you. Later we'll work on how to show emotions and actions without saying a word."

His lips turned down and he frowned, then he gave a loud sniffle. "And it is very hard to make me laugh."

All the other kids jumped up and raced toward the trunk. Michelle slowly wandered after them. She didn't feel like trying to be funny. Not today.

When it was Michelle's turn to pick a costume, there wasn't much left. She pulled out an ugly orange and green dress. It looked like something a little girl would wear in an old TV show. Something her dad watched when *he* was little. She pulled it on over her T-shirt and shorts.

"Here," Naomi said, giggling. "This will look perfect with your dress." She pinned a gigantic red bow to the top of Michelle's head.

Michelle looked into the tall mirror. "I look like a Christmas present with that bow on my head."

Naomi and a few of the kids giggled.

But Michelle didn't feel funny. She trudged over to the table and pulled a nose out of the box. She stuck it on.

Then she pulled a slip of paper out of the hat. *Susie's Sunny Day,* it said.

Oh, great, she thought. Now I'm supposed to act extra happy! When Mr. Hackman asked for volunteers, Michelle didn't raise her hand.

Michelle couldn't pay attention while the other kids did their skits. She kept picturing Katrina doing somersaults in the air—with Alexi catching her at the last second.

Why couldn't I even try? Michelle thought for the millionth time.

"Your turn," Mr. Hackman called to Michelle.

She shuffled to the front of the class. Her shoulders slumped. She couldn't think of *anything* to do. She wasn't feeling even a tiny bit funny.

"What's the name of your skit?" Mr. Hackman asked. He smiled at her.

Michelle couldn't help giving a big, big sigh. " 'Susie's Sunny Day,' " she answered.

A few kids in the class laughed.

I better get this over with, Michelle thought.

"It is such a sunny day. The world is a beautiful place," she said.

Michelle tried to sound happy, but all she could think was that she would never have another chance on the trapeze.

Michelle felt tears sting her eyes. She blinked them away. "I'm so happy . . ." she said.

It came out sounding really sad.

The class and Mr. Hackman burst out laughing.

Huh? They must think I'm acting sad on purpose—as a joke! I'll just make that my skit, Michelle thought. I'll be the saddest clown ever.

Michelle spotted an umbrella in the costume box and picked it up. "There's not a cloud in the sky," she said. "So I'd better take my umbrella."

Everyone laughed harder.

Michelle popped open her umbrella. The spring inside the handle broke and the umbrella closed on her head.

"Stupid umbrella," Michelle grumbled.

Michelle heard more laughter. Everyone seemed to love her grumpy Susie.

When she tried to put the umbrella back up, it turned inside out.

Michelle shook her head and tossed the umbrella back in the trunk. "Maybe I'll just go back to bed."

The whole class clapped and laughed.

"Okay, time for lunch, everyone," Mr. Hackman announced. "Put your costumes back in the box."

The teacher hurried over to Michelle. "You were great, Michelle," he said.

Michelle shrugged. "I didn't really plan it or anything."

"Some people are just naturally funny. And I think you're one of them," Mr. Hackman said. "Everything else—the makeup, the tricks—these things can be learned. But to be truly funny, to make people laugh— that's a gift you're born with."

He gave her big red bow a playful yank. "I think you'd make a wonderful clown in the show."

Naomi dragged Michelle up to the bulletin board. "I can't wait to see what my assignment is for the big show," Naomi said.

Michelle was afraid to look. She squeezed her eyes closed.

Maybe I wasn't as bad as I thought in trapeze, she told herself. It's probably normal to be scared at first. Maybe Katrina's parents saw some hidden talent in me. . . .

If they hadn't, maybe Madame Florence picked me for the dog act. That could be sort of fun. Michelle did like Fifi and Gerard.

Even bareback riding or juggling would be okay, she thought.

But please, please, please, don't let me be a clown.

She told everyone she was going to be a trapeze artist in the show. She couldn't end up as a grumpy, grouchy clown. She couldn't.

Michelle forced herself to open her eyes. She studied the list. Naomi got picked for bareback rider.

"You're going to be great," Michelle told her friend. "You were awesome that day in class."

Michelle studied the list again. She found her name. Her assignment was written there in big black letters.

Michelle Tanner—clown!

Chapter

8

♥ "I thought the show would be the best day of my life," Michelle mumbled. "Now I know it's going to be the worst."

Naomi put an arm around Michelle's shoulder. "Oh, Michelle, Don't feel bad. You'll make a great clown. You were so funny in class."

Michelle knew Naomi was trying to make her feel better. But it wasn't helping.

I need to talk to Dad, Michelle thought. Or Uncle Jesse or Aunt Becky. Or Joey. Or Steph. Or D.J.

I just need to talk to *someone* in my family. They can always cheer me up.

"I want to go back to the trailer for a little bit. I'll see you at lunch, okay?" Michelle told Naomi.

"Sure," Naomi said. "If I get there first, I'll save you a seat."

Michelle hurried to the pay phone near the front gate. She looked around. No one was nearby. Good. She didn't want anyone to hear her phone call.

Maybe I'll ask if I can go home, Michelle thought. Yes, she decided, that is what she really wanted to do.

She dropped in a quarter and dialed. "Please be home," she whispered.

"Hello?"

"Dad!" Michelle shouted. "It's me— Michelle!"

"Hi, sweetheart!" her father replied. It made her feel so much better to hear his voice. "How's it going? We miss you."

"I miss you, too," Michelle said. "Dad, can I talk to you about something—"

"Hey!" Michelle heard someone say in the background. "Is that Michelle? Can I talk to her?"

"Uh, sure," Danny said. "Michelle, hang on—"

"Michelle? Hi, it's Stephanie. I bet you're having a fabulous time, aren't you?"

"Well . . ."

"I hear you have a big bet going with Lee," her sister said with a giggle.

"Where did you hear about that?" Michelle asked.

"Oh, I heard some kids talking about it at the pool," Stephanie told her.

Oh, great, Michelle thought.

"Dad wants the phone back," Stephanie said. "See you next Saturday!"

Her dad came back on. "I bet you're having a great time, aren't you?"

"Well, actually, Dad—"

"Who wouldn't?" her dad went on. "Oh, Michelle, Uncle Jesse wants to speak to you."

"Hey, Michelle," Uncle Jesse said. "How's circus camp?"

"It's—"

"It's all Nicky and Alex can talk about," Uncle Jesse rushed on. "They're telling all their friends at day camp that they're going to a real circus. They're telling everybody that their cousin is a big circus star. Isn't that cute?"

"Really?" Michelle said. "Everybody?"

"Well, sure," Uncle Jesse said. "They're proud of you. We all are. Well, I've got to go. See you Saturday."

Then her father got back on the phone. "Uncle Jesse's right, Michelle. We're all so excited to see you perform. It's at two o'clock, right?"

"Uh, right," Michelle said. "But, Dad—"

"We're taking two cars so your friends can ride with us, too." He chuckled. "You'll probably have the biggest cheering section of all."

Michelle groaned.

If only he would slow down a little. If only he'd stop sounding so happy, then maybe she could tell him how miserable she was.

Ding!

"Oops! That's my timer, Michelle," her dad said. "I've got some carrot bread in the oven. Was there anything else you wanted to say?"

Michelle sighed. How could she say what she really wanted to say? How could she tell her father she wanted to quit and come home?

"Uh, nothing, Dad," Michelle said at last. "I just wanted to say hi. I'm having a great time. See you Saturday."

Then she hung up. She sat there, staring at her reflection in the metal of the pay phone.

"There's no way I can be a clown with everyone coming to see me," she whispered. "No way am I going to let Lee win our bet."

Somehow she'd have to get the circus teachers to change their minds.

Somehow she was going to conquer her fear of heights.

Somehow, some way, I'm going to be on that trapeze Saturday night!

Chapter

9

♥ Michelle wandered back toward her trailer. She still had a half hour of free time before lunch.

As she passed the main building, she saw all the Amazing Novaks standing near one of the trapeze ladders.

Michelle took a deep breath and hurried inside. She headed straight for Katrina.

"Uh, can I talk to you for a minute?" she asked.

"Sure," Katrina said. She led Michelle over to the bleachers, and they sat down.

"I want to be a trapeze artist in the show,"

Michelle blurted out. "Will you help me practice?"

Katrina shook her head. "But, Michelle, the decisions about the show have already been made."

"Please, Katrina," Michelle begged. "I told all my friends and family back home I was going to fly on the trapeze. Help me, please? I can stop being afraid of heights. I'm sure of it.

"Then I can practice and get better," Michelle continued. "And if I get better, maybe I can still get the teachers to change their minds. Maybe I can still fly on the trapeze."

"I don't know if the teachers will change their minds even if you do get better," Katrina said. "But if you want to try, I'll help you. Come on."

Katrina and Michelle rushed over to Mr. and Mrs. Novak and Alexi.

"Michelle really wants to give the trapeze another try," Katrina told her parents.

"Would you work the safety lines so I can practice with her?"

"Of course we'll help the little birdie learn to fly," Mr. Novak said. He and Mrs. Novak helped Michelle into the safety belt.

Michelle marched over to the bottom of the ladder and stared up. Katrina and Alexi stood behind her.

"So, were you ever afraid?" she asked Katrina and her brother.

"Afraid?" Alexi scoffed. "Never! Flying is in our blood."

Katrina rolled her eyes. "It's not that simple, Alexi, and you know it. And, yes, Michelle, sometimes I am afraid when I'm learning a new trick. My grandmother was a flyer, too. And you know what she used to say?"

Katrina's voice changed, and she spoke like a little old woman with a foreign accent. "Afraid? Of course you are afraid! A little bit of fear is good. Without the fear, you get lazy. You don't pay attention. Then—boom!—you fall down, break your neck!"

Michelle laughed at Katrina's imitation. "I get it."

Michelle remembered something from juggling. "Hey, maybe I need to start by juggling one ball."

"Huh?" Alexi scratched his head. "If you juggle on the trapeze, you'll definitely fall!"

"No, no," Michelle said, laughing. "Charley told my class that we had to break juggling into easy little steps. He told us to start juggling with one ball, then two, then three."

Michelle thought for a moment. "On the trapeze, I'll start with the ladder. I'll work on climbing all the way to the platform without being scared."

She put her foot on the first step of the ladder and began to climb. When she reached the fourth step, she stopped, looked at the ground, and then climbed back down.

"That wasn't too bad," she said.

She started back up the ladder again.

"Now try a little higher," Katrina encouraged her. "Don't worry, I'll be right here."

This time Michelle climbed halfway up and down. She took it slowly.

"You're doing great, Michelle!" Katrina said. Alexi gave her a thumbs-up.

"It's a lot easier when you don't have a whole class staring at you," she answered.

Michelle started up the ladder again. A few more steps, she coached herself. Now a few more. Then a few more.

I'm there! Michelle reached out and touched the platform. Then she started to climb back down.

No, she decided. I think I'm ready to do more. I'm going all the way up.

She climbed up onto the platform. "Whoo-hoo!" she shouted.

Then she glanced down. Whoops! She clung to the pole and closed her eyes.

She took a deep breath. Then she opened her eyes.

She still felt nervous, but she didn't feel as scared as before!

She hurried down the ladder and gave Katrina a hug. "It's getting easier!" Michelle exclaimed.

"Time for lunch, kids," Mrs. Novak called.

"Thanks so much for helping me, everyone," Michelle said.

"Come by tomorrow after your classes and we can practice some more," Katrina said.

"At the big show on Saturday, it isn't enough just to act goofy." Mr. Hackman walked up and down in front of the kids who would be clowns in the show.

"Don't just slip on a banana peel and fall down," he continued. "Anybody can do that! Create a character. Then tell a story. You want to make the audience care about you. *That's* what makes a good clown."

I'm not going to be a clown on Saturday, Michelle promised herself. But I'm in this class today, so I might as well have fun, she thought.

"Okay, everyone, into your costumes," Mr. Hackman called.

Michelle and the other kids hurried over to the big black trunk. Maybe I can find something better than the orange and green dress I wore last time, she thought.

"Hey, how do I look?" Alice, one of the other girls in the class, asked. She held up her foot so Michelle could get a look at her sneakers. They looked twice as big as Michelle's dad's shoes.

"They're fantastic," Michelle answered.

"Don't you just love being a clown?" Alice asked.

"I don't really want to be a clown," Michelle admitted. "I want to be a trapeze artist."

Michelle spotted a shiny pink ballet costume in the trunk. It was covered with sparkly sequins—and full of holes. She pulled it on.

She gave a big sigh. "I want to wear a beautiful costume. I want to fly through the air."

Michelle heard laughter and turned around.

A few kids stood there watching her. They think I'm working on my act, Michelle thought. That gives me a great idea!

Michelle giggled. She grabbed a headdress with three drooping feathers. She perched it on her head.

She stuck on a rubber nose and bowed to the group of kids.

Then she pretended to climb a ladder. She pretended to grab hold of a trapeze bar and swing through the air.

She knew she looked silly in her ragged costume and fake nose. Especially when she slipped on the tile floor and landed on her backside.

That really made the kids laugh.

Michelle put her hands on her hips and scowled at them. Then she dusted off her costume. She adjusted the feathers on her headdress.

Mr. Hackman wandered over. He was laughing, too.

He gave her a big bow. "I did not catch your name, beautiful lady."

"I didn't throw it," Michelle shot back, batting her eyes at him.

"Excellent, Michelle," Mr. Hackman exclaimed. "You must work on this character and do it for the show."

Mr. Hackman sounded so happy.

How am I going to tell him I don't want to be a clown? Michelle thought.

Chapter 10

♥ As soon as clown class let out, Michelle ran straight to the trapeze. She didn't even bother to change out of her costume.

Mr. and Mrs. Novak helped her into her safety belt.

"Are you going to try swinging today?" Alexi asked her.

Michelle glanced up at the bar high, high above her. She shook her head. "I want to spend one more day on the ladder," she said. "I don't want to look even a teeny bit nervous when I climb up."

Alexi snorted.

"I think that's a great idea, Michelle," Katrina said. "Mom and Dad always say the show starts with the very first step up the ladder. You should practice smiling to the audience when you climb."

Michelle nodded. Then she started up the ladder. She didn't look down. She hardly felt nervous at all. She turned her head toward the bleachers and gave her biggest smile.

I have to tell Charley he should start teaching the trapeze instead of juggling, Michelle thought.

"More smiling practice?" Alexi asked Michelle two days later. "Aren't your lips getting tired?"

"Don't listen to him," Mrs. Novak said as she checked Michelle's safety lines. "Alexi loves to tease."

"That's for sure," Katrina answered.

"But, um, maybe you should try swinging today," she added softly. "Today the kids who are doing the trapeze act in the show worked on swinging from one platform to the next. You don't want to get too far behind them."

"You're right," Michelle agreed. "Today I'll swing."

I have to, Michelle thought. The teachers will never agree to let me be a trapeze artist in the show if I can't keep up with the other kids.

"Great! I'll meet you on the platform," Katrina said. She started up the ladder.

Michelle followed her. She didn't have to think about each step anymore. Also, her hands didn't get sweaty or anything.

She climbed up onto the platform next to Katrina. The platform didn't seem quite so tiny now. Or *quite* so high.

Michelle waved to Alexi. He stood on the opposite platform. "I'm ready!" she called.

Alexi nodded and sent the trapeze bar flying toward her.

Michelle took a deep breath. It was now or never.

I'm going to do it! she told herself.

She grabbed the bar.

Now go!

Michelle felt her feet leave the platform. The air whistled past her ears as she swung out over the net. Her stomach flip-flopped.

Wow! I'm doing it!

I'm really flying!

"Now pump your legs, and you'll be able to swing yourself over to me," Alexi called. "I'll help you onto the platform."

Michelle tried, but couldn't move her legs. They felt frozen.

Just don't look down, she told herself. Don't look down, don't look down, don't look down. . . .

Michelle looked down.

Then her hands slipped from the trapeze bar.

Down, down, down she fell. . . .

"NOOO!" Michelle screamed.

Boing!

Michelle bounced into the net.

She popped into the air and landed in the net again.

Then she gave three more tiny bounces.

Michelle felt as if she'd just taken a ride on the world's biggest roller coaster.

She took a deep breath and stared up at the trapeze platform.

What am I going to do? Michelle thought. The other kids are already swinging all the way from one platform to the other.

I can't even hang on to the bar!

She struggled to sit up. Katrina and Alexi stood next to the net, laughing at her.

Laughing! Michelle couldn't believe it.

"It's not funny!" Michelle cried.

"I—I'm sorry, Michelle," Katrina gasped, trying hard to stop laughing. "We're not laughing at you because you fell. It was just so funny—you flying through the air in that clown suit."

But I want to look beautiful as I soar through the air, Michelle thought. I don't want to look funny. This isn't clown class.

Wait a minute! she thought. That gives me a great idea!

Chapter 11

♥ Michelle and Naomi peeked into the audience.

"There's my family," Michelle whispered. "Right there in the second row."

"All those people?" Naomi asked.

"Well, most of them," Michelle answered. "Except for those three. They're my friends." She pointed to Cassie and Mandy and Lee.

Daniel hurried over to them. "Time to get ready, Naomi," he said. "Spotty is waiting for you."

Michelle gave Naomi a hug. "Good luck! I know you're going to be great."

"You, too!" Naomi said.

Michelle hurried back to the girls' dressing room. Her act was last. She didn't know how she would wait so long for her turn.

"Welcome to the Golden State Junior Circus," Michelle heard the ringmaster call in his deep, low voice. "Our performers have been working hard to put on a very special show for you."

Michelle started to feel a little nervous. Would her friends and family be surprised at her act? Would they like it?

I wish I could watch the show until it's my turn, Michelle thought.

At least she could listen. She heard the ringmaster announce Naomi. Then she heard the sound of Spotty's hooves as he thundered around the ring.

Michelle held her breath until she heard the audience cheering. I knew Naomi would be great, she thought.

Michelle listened to Fifi and Gerard's part

of the show. She could picture the two poodles running their obstacle course.

She listened to the juggling act and heard only one *thud!*

She listened to the ooohs and aaahs during the trapeze act. I hope people like my act that much, she thought.

Finally it was Michelle's turn. She checked her fake nose. She straightened her orange and green dress.

"I hope I can make this work," she whispered. Then she stepped into the center ring carrying a beat-up suitcase.

She stopped in the spotlight. She turned and stared up at the trapeze with longing. She blew it a kiss. She exaggerated her actions so everyone in the audience could see what she was doing.

Then she opened her suitcase. The crowd laughed as she pulled out the pink sequined costume with all the holes.

Michelle hugged it to her chest as if it were the most beautiful costume in the world. Then she slipped it on—right over her clown clothes. Pieces of her orange and green dress stuck out the holes.

Next she put on the headdress with the droopy feathers. She held up a mirror to check herself out.

Smack! She gave her image in the mirror a noisy kiss.

The audience laughed harder.

As Mr. and Mrs. Novak put on her safety belt and harness, beautiful music from the ballet *Swan Lake* began to play.

Michelle hurried toward the ladder leading up to the trapeze. She climbed three steps, then hurried back down. She knocked her knees together and pretended to bite her nails.

She heard lots of giggles from the crowd.

Michelle started up the ladder again. When she reached the platform, Alexi winked at her. Michelle winked back.

Then she started to bow to the audience. Her mouth dropped open when she saw how far down they were. She fell to her knees and clung to the platform.

She started back toward the ladder—and froze. She shook her head back and forth. She wanted everyone to know she was way too scared to climb back down.

As the audience laughed and laughed, Michelle scooted back up to the platform and hugged the pole closely.

Katrina waved to Michelle from the opposite platform. She swung the bar out to Michelle.

Michelle stared at the ground, and pretended not to notice the trapeze.

On the third swing Michelle held her hands up and pretended to grab on to the bar accidentally. Alexi gave her a push, and with a squeal she swung out over the net.

Michelle opened her mouth in a silent scream.

Then Michelle's right hand slipped from the bar. She squealed.

The audience stopped laughing. People gasped!

Michelle held her nose as if she were about to dive underwater.

Then her left hand slipped from the bar.

Michelle was falling!

Chapter

12

♥ *Boing!*

Michelle bounced up and down in the net.

When she stopped bouncing, she lay still. The audience was completely silent.

Then she shakily climbed out of the net.

The audience held its breath as she stumbled to the center of the ring.

With a huge smile Michelle made a dramatic bow. To the right. To the left. To the center.

Then she took a deep breath—and pretended to faint dead away!

Thump! The sawdust rose around her as she tumbled to the ground.

The audience burst into laughter and applause.

Michelle lay in the sawdust and smiled.

I did it, she thought. I made them laugh. And I flew on the trapeze, too.

Michelle ran backstage and joined the rest of the performers. When the ringmaster gave the signal, they marched out into the center ring for the final parade.

Everyone in the crowd smiled and waved as they walked by. Michelle spotted her family and blew them a big kiss.

After the parade, Michelle rushed outside. She couldn't wait to see her family and Cassie and Mandy and Lee.

"There she is," she heard her dad yell. A second later he swooped her up in a big hug.

"Michelle, you were great," Mandy said.

Uncle Jesse held up a video camera. "I got the whole thing on tape."

Nicky and Alex pulled on her arms.

"Can I try on your nose?" Nicky asked.

"Will you teach us how to be clowns?" Alex begged.

"Of course," Michelle said, giving them both hugs.

"I should have known you would make everyone laugh," her father said proudly. "You've always been such a clown—even when you were little."

"Really?" Michelle said.

"Oh, yeah, you're the funniest one in the family," Joey said. "Next to me, of course."

Everyone laughed.

Aunt Becky gave Michelle a big hug and a bunch of flowers. "Congratulations, Michelle."

"Thanks," Michelle exclaimed.

"You were awesome," Cassie said. She turned around and jabbed Lee in the ribs. "Right, Lee?"

Uh-oh, Michelle thought. What about their bet?

"Well," Lee grumbled. "Michelle's act wasn't exactly what I expected."

"But she did go on the trapeze," Mandy reminded him. "In a sparkly costume. Right?"

"Right," Lee admitted.

He grinned at Michelle. "I have to admit it," he said. "You were really cool. I guess you win our bet after all."

"Thanks, Lee." Michelle grinned. "I hope you've got your pajamas and teddy bear ready."

FULL HOUSE™

Club Stephanie

Stephanie and her friends are looking forward to a summer full of sailing fun! There's just one problem: the super-rotten, super-snooty group called the Flamingoes....

Too Many Flamingoes
(Coming mid-May 1998)

Friend or Flamingo?
(Coming mid-June 1998)

Flamingoes Overboard!
(Coming mid-July 1998)

Collect all three books in this brand-new trilogy!

Based on the hit Warner Bros. TV series

 A MINSTREL® BOOK

Published by Pocket Books

1357-02

FULL HOUSE Stephanie™

 Available from Minstrel® Books Published by Pocket Books

FULL HOUSE™
Michelle

#5: THE GHOST IN MY CLOSET 53573-0/$3.99

#6: BALLET SURPRISE 53574-9/$3.99

#7: MAJOR LEAGUE TROUBLE 53575-7/$3.99

#8: MY FOURTH-GRADE MESS 53576-5/$3.99

#9: BUNK 3, TEDDY, AND ME 56834-5/$3.99

**#10: MY BEST FRIEND IS A MOVIE STAR!
(Super Edition) 56835-3/$3.99**

#11: THE BIG TURKEY ESCAPE 56836-1/$3.99

#12: THE SUBSTITUTE TEACHER 00364-X/$3.99

#13: CALLING ALL PLANETS 00365-8/$3.99

#14: I'VE GOT A SECRET 00366-6/$3.99

#15: HOW TO BE COOL 00833-1/$3.99

#16: THE NOT-SO-GREAT OUTDOORS 00835-8/$3.99

#17: MY HO-HO-HORRIBLE CHRISTMAS 00836-6/$3.99

**MY AWESOME HOLIDAY FRIENDSHIP BOOK
(An Activity Book) 00840-4/$3.99**

FULL HOUSE MICHELLE OMNIBUS 02181-8/$6.99

#18: MY ALMOST PERFECT PLAN 00837-4/$3.99

#19: APRIL FOOLS 01729-2/$3.99

A MINSTREL® BOOK
Published by Pocket Books